PRAISE FOR

Top 10 Romance of 2012, 2015, and 2016.

— BOOKLIST: THE NIGHT IS MINE, HOT POINT,
HEART STRIKE

One of our favorite authors.

— RT BOOK REVIEWS

Buchman has catapulted his way to the top tier of my favorite authors.

— FRESH FICTION

A favorite author of mine. I'll read anything that carries his name, no questions asked. Meet your new favorite author!

— THE SASSY BOOKSTER, FLASH OF FIRE

M.L. Buchman is guaranteed to get me lost in a good story.

— THE READING CAFE, WAY OF THE WARRIOR:
NSDQ

I love Buchman's writing. His vivid descriptions bring everything to life in an unforgettable way.

DELTA MISSION: OPERATION RUDOLPH

A DELTA FORCE ROMANCE STORY

M. L. BUCHMAN

Buchman Bookworks

Other works by M. L. Buchman:

CHAPTER 1

*L*ive-fire training.

    She didn't need any blasted live-fire training. Especially not during a freak snowstorm that was inundating Range 37 at Fort Bragg, North Carolina. Betsy's personal thermostat was currently set to Congo jungle, not three-days-before-Christmas blizzard.

Okay, the pretty white flakes fluttering down on the rifle range didn't count as a blizzard—though she'd grown up in Arkansas and it was more than she was used to—but it was cold enough that they were sticking to everything, including her. And her breath showed in puffs. She focused on breathing only through her nose to cut down on the clouds that might give away her position to the instructors.

The fact that she was out of Delta Force and the Army in three more days didn't matter to them. She'd done her decade in the field and Christmas Day would mark her release from service. But when command said you did a training, you did one. She was theirs to order about until the moment she walked out the gate.

Betsy kept low behind a stone wall and pondered the

enemy's next move. She'd barely had a glimpse of the artificial town that was the core of the training range's purpose. The Fort Bragg training squadron was always rearranging it in unexpected ways. She'd been in the field for a full year on her latest deployment, so the hundreds of hours she'd spent here over the years were now irrelevant.

The hundred-plus acres of Range 37 was a 360-degree, live-fire shoothouse. Some parts were modern urban, others Kandahar Province-low-and-crammed-together.

What kind of idiot training scenario sent a solo soldier on a snatch-and-grab mission? Minimum for that type of operation was a four-man team: two to grab, two to guard. Instead, they'd sent her in on her own without any explanation.

The only way out is through. Old axiom.

Of course solo was the story of her life. Dad gone from the beginning. While her high school classmates had been discovering friends and sex, she'd been caring for her mother through a fatal bout of cancer. Delta Force, the true loners of the US military, had been as natural to her as breathing. One of the only women there? Sure. Whatever.

But a one-woman snatch-and-grab operation? She was probably the best they had for that—no matter how stupid an idea it was. Perhaps they were using her to test some crazy scenario just to see how it worked.

Fine! Time to show them just what she *could* do.

She lay down in the snow and fast-rolled across the gap between the stone wall she'd been crouched behind and the brick building next over. As she rolled, she kept her rifle scope to her eye. Her best moving shot for rooftops was actually on her back, not her stomach—an unlikely trick she'd learned by accident in Mosul. Head tipped back, HK416 at the ready, she spotted two hostiles atop the wall on the far side of a broad courtyard. She hit both from her back, rolled onto her stomach, double-tapped an armed bad guy target crouching by a plywood maple tree, then two more into the mannequins on the roof from her back just to make sure the targets stayed dead.

The six hard clangs of bullets striking metal targets registered only after she was safe behind the red brick.

She held her fire as two children mannequins peeked at her from a nearby window. A dummy woman rushed across the street, her form gliding on a hidden track. A rough-painted man close behind her, using the woman figure as a shield, had an AK-47. Two harsh rings of metal echoed between the buildings as Betsy shot him twice in the face—all she could see of him—and one more as she hit his knee through the fluttering back of the woman's dress.

A particularly large snowflake plastered itself across the lens of her shooting goggles. It left a wet smear when she brushed it aside.

Betsy had tracked her quarry off the edge of the map somewhere, slipping out of simulated Afghanistan into a quaint French village setting that she didn't recall ever seeing before.

The next building over, probably just painted plywood, was an exceptional imitation of rose-and-gray stonework, medieval arches, and cobbled streets barely wide enough for two donkeys to pass. It would make a resting place for the Merovingian French kings back before the Dark Ages. With the snow, it looked perfect for finding a little Provençal bistro with a mug of mulled wine and a cozy chair by a stone fireplace.

Of course the best that would be waiting for her after this would be a hot cup of coffee and a burger at the SWCS DFAC—the Special Warfare Center and School Dining Facility. If she didn't freeze to death first.

A glance back the way she'd come to make sure no one was behind her and—

Betsy blinked hard, as if that would clear away the obscuring snow.

There was no longer an Afghan town behind her, though she knew she'd just been through one. She was at the center of a French village that looked too authentic, even for Range 37. Alleys twisted. Yew trees, so old and gnarled they truly might have been planted by some ancient French king, rose before a two-story, stone, row house. A cluster of dormant rose vines climbed a nearby wall, some of the stems thicker than her arm. They'd been there a while…a long while.

An actual donkey, pulling a tiny cart bearing a large wine barrel, clopped along, his unshod hooves muffled by the fallen snow. The hard rattle of the two ironclad, wooden wheels sounded from the cobbles.

She spun back to look down the street where she'd just shot the target with an AK-47. More people flowed across the courtyard now, but not gliding on any hidden rail. Some carried gigantic woven baskets, others wooden platters of food—all hurrying this way and that as if preparing for some event. Their clothing was loose and broadcloth.

And puffs of breath were coming out of their mouths.

There weren't supposed to be any real people in a live-fire training except the attackers—in this scenario, just her. If she made a mistake, she could kill an innocent, not that she ever had. She'd always scored perfect marks in target discernment. A man came out a doorway close beside where she lay in the snow and almost stepped on her.

"Excusez-moi." He definitely spoke before hurrying down the road. Not a mannequin.

She sat up carefully, keeping her eye out for potential shooters. All of the people on the streets—and there were more with each passing moment—were dressed for some form of medieval village reenactment like the Norwegian Folk Museum in Oslo, only more French-Grand-Master-painting-come-to-life than simplistic-Nordic.

Not a one looked at her. She glanced down at herself to be sure that she hadn't changed as well. Army boots, camo pants, Kevlar shooter's vest filled with spare magazines for her rifle and a Glock still in its holster. She indeed still held her HK416 rifle and could feel the helmet on her head. Another blink, and she could feel her eyelashes brushing on the inside of her shooter goggles.

"What the hell?"

Even the air smelled different. Baked breads, wood fires, roasting meat that made her stomach growl.

Only one man was out of place now. He stood in the exact center of the courtyard and was looking directly at her.

Out of place! The alarm went off in her head. Instinct kicked in and she aimed and fired, only at the last moment realizing that he held no weapon. She tried to shift her aim, but knew it wasn't enough.

The man leaned slightly to one side and the bullet missed his cheek by a hair's breadth, smacking into a stone arch behind him and releasing a puff of rock dust as it pulverized itself.

Then, as calm as could be, he looked back at her.

Nobody, but nobody dodged a round fired from an HK416.

CHAPTER 2

*B*etsy could only stare at him as the villagers continued to mill about without paying any attention to either of them. By now the donkey had drawn even with her position. She reached out to touch it. Though she wore thin gloves, it felt real enough.

The man, however, didn't look real. Six feet tall, but slender as a willow branch. He didn't look unfit or misproportioned, just impossibly slender. He had glorious black hair that fell to his waist, whereas her own blonde was short-cropped and barely reached her jawline. He had a long face with high cheekbones, pale skin, and the bluest eyes she'd ever seen. He was dressed in form-fitting black leather that might be appropriate for a chick on a motorcycle calendar. It did look very fine on him, so maybe she finally understood why guys went so ape over those kinds of calendars. A little. Not much really.

One thing was for certain, though. It made him look even more out of place in Medieval France than she did.

She couldn't react, couldn't find it in her to move as he

stepped among the hurrying townsfolk until he was standing just an arm's-length away. A thin red line scored his cheek.

He noticed the direction of her attention and raised a hand to brush at it.

"I'll have to remember to move faster in future encounters."

"Move. Faster." People didn't step aside from bullets moving at 890 meters per second.

His smile was brief, but dazzling and she could only blink in surprise.

"But..." She didn't know "but" what, but it was the only sound she could make.

"I'm Horatio."

"Horatio?"

"Yes," his voice was impossibly deep and sounded more like flowing water than spoken words.

"Is that like 'Go West, Young Man' Horatio Alger? Or 'Alas, poor Yorick' in Hamlet?"

"Nor Captain Horatio Hornblower. Just Horatio the Herder."

"The herder of what? Who..." No. "*What* are you?" She forced herself to look away from his dazzling blue eyes. Her gaze landed on a prominently pointed ear where the chill wind blew aside an elegant length of his hair like some runway model's. He was both the handsomest and the prettiest man she'd ever seen, even if he wasn't one.

A group of children, ones she'd have labeled as beggars, gathered together in a group and began to sing in Latin. As a child, she'd chosen to do her confirmation into the Roman Catholic church in Latin. As an adult, she could only wonder why she'd bothered with any of it.

Orientis partibus
adventavit asinus,

pulcher et fortissimus,
Sarcinis aptissimus.

"From the east, the pretty Advent donkey carries the sacred baggage?" Maybe not so much with her Catholic school Latin.

"It is an ancient Latin Christmas carol, popular in twelfth-century France," the man waved his long-fingered hand negligently about as if that was somehow where they were. "In your language it is called *The Friendly Beasts* and relates the legend of the animals who helped with the birth of Jesus. That verse is the donkey telling of carrying Mary to the manger."

"Oh." What else was she supposed to say to such a crazy statement. She considered for a moment. This *definitely* wasn't Range 37. She rose to her toes and tried clicking the heels of her Army boots together three times.

Nothing changed.

Maybe it only worked for ruby Army boots.

Horatio smiled at her as if he knew exactly what she was doing.

"Allow me to escort you elsewhere," he turned sideways to her and offered his arm. At a loss for what else to do, she shifted her rifle to her other hand—in shooting, all Delta operators were ambidextrous— left the safety off, and slipped her fingers about his elbow. He felt as thin as he looked, but he felt as strong as a seasoned operator who could hike fifty kilometers with a full pack, just to get *into* battle.

He led her down the street to a doorway that had a wooden sign hung above it depicting a cluster of grapes, and led her inside. The smoke from the big, ill-vented, stone fireplace stung her eyes and there was a rank smell like an entire Delta platoon that had been in the field for a month without bathing. But beneath that, the cinnamon and nutmeg of mulled wine and the richness of mutton stew filled the air.

Horatio sat with the elegance of a powerful man at a small, rough table close by the warm fire. She propped her rifle against the wall close to hand and sat across from him. Their knees brushed together comfortably. He didn't draw away, but neither did he press. It was merely comfortable, friendly even. Not something she was used to with men. For the most part they either wanted sex or wanted her to get the hell out of the boys' club military unit. Horatio the Herder was harder to read and she rather liked that bit of mystery.

In moments, they were served with clay mugs of wine— enough to plow her under the table if she tried to finish it— and a steaming bowl of stew.

"The wine is quite acceptable, but I would exercise a degree of caution regarding the stew," Horatio winced as if it was bad memory.

She sipped at the wine and decided that if *this* was good wine, she'd definitely be avoiding the stew.

Betsy pinched herself, no change.

"Any chance that you'd know how badly I was injured or when I'm getting off these drugs? Or are you just a gorgeous hallucination named Horatio?"

Horatio hid a smile with a big draught of wine, but his blue eyes twinkled. They *actually* twinkled. It made him look very merry. If he really was in full elf-character, which his pointy ears indicated was likely, maybe it was part of his job to be merry. But that didn't explain how he'd made those pretty blue eyes twinkle. Of course "Elf: identification and interaction with" wasn't in any part of Delta Force's Operator Training Course.

Maybe she didn't want off these drugs, whatever they were. She'd had morphine after being shot up in Nigeria once and been completely loopy but calm as well. She still remembered portions of that helo ride while the combat search-and-rescue medics struggled to stabilize her. An incredibly handsome stranger, even in a seedy medieval pub, was a far more interesting reaction.

"I can place you back in Range 37 at any moment you should choose to request it. But I would like to discuss a special mission with you prior to such an eventuality."

"A special mission?" She tried the wine again while considering where he might have learned such speech patterns. British sit-coms came to mind. The second sip of wine slammed the back of her throat with its tannic bite. This time it only made her want to gag rather than rip her throat out, which was an improvement. She could also taste the high alcohol content. That, she decided, could be a good thing in the current situation and managed to brace herself through a third taste, but couldn't manage a fourth.

"Yes," Horatio spooned up some of the stew, apparently ignoring his earlier warning—at least until he put it in his mouth. Then looked as if he didn't know where to spit it out.

"In the fire."

He did so, creating a brief flurry of sparks.

"Back to my question," Betsy nudged her own stew bowl a little farther away as a safety precaution. "What *are* you and why am I hallucinating you?"

Not finding anywhere to wipe his mouth, he used his fingers, then wiped them on the edge of the table. "You are *not* hallucinating."

"Just what I'd expect a hallucination to say."

Horatio sighed before forging on. "This is real. Or mostly real. We see each other, but the locals merely observe a pair of strangers in locals' clothing."

"Uh-huh." Betsy could only assume this was one of those accidents that was bad enough for amnesia to kick in. Most of this she wouldn't mind losing, though Horatio himself was a real pleasure to look at. She'd been in the field a long time and dallying with a squad mate just wasn't an option. Horatio however… He looked far yummier than the wine.

What *had* happened?

Maybe a stone wall of Range 37 collapsed onto her? Or perhaps one of her shots at the metal targets had ricocheted back. At this point it wouldn't surprise if one of the targets had *shot* her back. Talking to a reindeer herding elf in a twelfth-century pub made anything seem possible.

"And as pertains to your earlier question, I am an elf—of the Christmas variety. The one entrusted with the care of Santa's reindeer, if I may be specific."

"Hence, Horatio the Herder," Betsy didn't think her imagination was strange enough to cook up this one, which was tipping the scale—impossibly—toward the side of this experience being somehow real.

"Precisely. My dilemma lies in the fact that it is only three days to Christmas and I can not find the lead reindeer anywhere. I have need of aid from a professional."

"Me?"

"You."

"You need me to track down…Rudolph?"

"Well, his name is Jeremy, but essentially yes."

"Jeremy the red-nosed reindeer. Doesn't exactly have the right ring to it, does it?"

"Robert L. May was prone to agreeing with you, which is why he changed the name for the Montgomery Ward children's book he wrote regarding Jeremy's tribulations as a young reindeer."

"Wow!" Betsy managed a large swallow of wine to fortify herself. "You actually delivered all that as a straight line. I'm impressed." Then she stared down at the wine and wondered what exactly was in it that she almost believed him.

CHAPTER 3

"*S*o, lay it out for me."

"Lay *it* out? What needs laying out of it?"

Betsy pulled out her Benchmade Infidel knife, thumbed the release, and the four-inch, double-edged blade snapped out the front of the handle. She began carving the Special Operations Command shoulder patch into the wooden table with the point—a stylized arrowhead with a knife up the middle.

Horatio eyed her carefully. "I expect that you are a hard woman to buy Christmas presents for. What's your Christmas wish?"

"I gave up on wishes a long time ago."

Horatio looked at her aghast.

She held up the blade. The black-coated D2 steel appeared bloody in the dim firelight. "This one did nicely as a gift to myself. Start talking, Elf." She returned to her carving.

"We permit the reindeer to run wild during the summer season."

"I could do with a little running wild myself." Betsy could

feel her inhibitions slipping away. She hadn't had that much wine. But knowing that you were injured and in some drug-induced dream made it difficult to care much about propriety. And if she was going to run a little wild, who better to do it with than a gorgeous man-elf-herder-thing.

"They always return when the fall lengthens the wavelengths that leaves reflect."

"Lengthens the wavelengths? Oh, reds and golds. Never mind. Keep going." Keeping her gaze averted from his intense eyes didn't help much. His slightly hoity-toity way of speaking didn't diminish the fact that his voice was just as beautiful as he was. She couldn't be so shallow that a beautiful man with a liquid voice was getting to her, even if he was.

"Jeremy has failed to return."

"That was the fall. And you're just contacting me three days before Christmas? That is not what we'd typically call adroit mission planning." She began digging the arch of the upper tab of the shoulder patch. What if she carved in the word "Airborne" as it should be and the table was discovered eight hundred years from now? Cause a hell of a stir. Perhaps she should drop into wherever this village was in the real world and find out for herself.

"Actually, yesterday was the final day of fall. We have now traversed the threshold of the winter solstice and such matters are suddenly come to a head."

"Maybe a hunter got him."

Horatio actually flinched. His oddly light complexion paled even further.

"Sorry, but you have to consider all of the possibilities."

"That is one I shall not be considering until all other hope is lost."

"So, where do we begin?" It wasn't often that an impossibly beautiful man asked her to do something so highly unlikely. Usually it was requests for sexual favors, which wasn't something she doled out to any Tom, Dick, or Horatio.

"At the stables, I suppose."

"Of course. Because why wouldn't Santa's reindeer have stables. Are you nuts, Horatio? I was thinking it was me, but maybe it's you."

"I have not considered the possibility," Horatio's beautiful brow actually furrowed for a long moment as he studied his wine, then shook his head, causing his hair to flutter attractively. "No, I find your premise unlikely."

Could she ever be with a man prettier than she was? If he looked like Horatio, in a heartbeat.

"Do elves kiss?" It was amazing what could be done within a drug-induced haze.

"We do," the color returned to his cheeks, brightly.

"Do they marry?"

"Is that a proposal, Betsy?"

Now it was her turn to scoff. "I just don't like my fantasies to already be married before I kiss them."

"Then you may do so without further concern if that is your wish." The bright color high on his cheeks wasn't going away, which was rather cute.

It would be a little like kissing a movie star. He was too perfect. But that wasn't exactly a complaint worth filing with the Fantasy Dream Department—a division of the US Army Personnel Services Branch she'd never thought of submitting a requisition request to before.

Betsy reached across the table to snag the lapel of his body-hugging black leather suit and pulled him closer. She leaned in and briefly tasted the mutton stew on his lips. Thankfully, she was past that before it could put her off completely. Past that, he tasted of cinnamon and the wild outdoors of a snowy night. Of luscious hot cocoa and a crackling fire.

Horatio's kiss was warm, attentive, thoughtful…and masterful.

If she hadn't been dreaming before, she most certainly was now. Dreaming of how fast they could go somewhere there weren't any other people, just the two of them and a big, warm bed.

Her pulse was soon chattering faster than an M134 Minigun on full auto, yet Horatio was still only exploring the first steps of a kiss.

"Get me out of here," her own voice sounded desperate and needy.

"As you wish."

CHAPTER 4

he cold slapped her so hard that she lost her breath—as well as her lip lock on Horatio.

"What the hell?"

"The stables."

"You brought me to a freezing cold barn?"

"I brought you to the source as you requested. These are the reindeer stables of St. Nicholas of Myra."

Betsy could only look around in astonishment. A long line of stalls appeared to be made out of living yew trees, all trained into walls and stable dividers. Their roots were lost beneath a luxuriant layer of living grass—the brightest green she'd ever seen. The stables were lit by fireflies swarming among the branches.

And the sky.

The ceiling was of glass so clear that she could hardly tell it was there between her and the magnificent night sky. As she blinked away the worst of the pub's smoke and her eyes adjusted, she began picking out constellations.

"That's the North Star."

Horatio looked up as well. "It is."

"It's directly overhead."

"Point six seven degrees from directly overhead to be precise. We are at the celestial north pole rather than the magnetic or geographic one. Nice, isn't it?"

"But the North Pole isn't over land. It's over sea ice."

"It is, in most planes of reality."

Betsy couldn't think of what else to do…so she hit him. Not hard—it had been a very nice kiss after all. Just squarely enough in the solar plexus that he wouldn't be able to speak for a few moments so that she could do some thinking.

Horatio dropped to his knees and wheezed a bit.

North Pole.

A missing reindeer named Jeremy.

An elf, a very handsome elf who could kiss better than any human—a kiss that also left her wondering what else he could do better.

St. Nicholas beneath Polaris the North Star in some very adjacent reality.

Real? Surreal? Digital? Drugs?

No way to tell.

She sighed, and helped Horatio back to his feet.

The only way out is through. Old axiom. There were times she hated old axioms.

"Last spring. Did anyone see which way Jeremy went?"

CHAPTER 5

*I*t had taken the CIA years to find bin Laden. And another half-year to actually get around to taking him down after "Maya" had found him.

She had three days to track a reindeer. Her total assets? One elf who didn't want it to be known that he'd lost Santa's most famous reindeer, Jeremy.

The first break came when they were questioning the other reindeer. They didn't like having her around and were very standoffish, until she dug around in Horatio's larder and found a bag of carrots. They warmed up to her quickly after that. Who knew that reindeer had a major weak spot for carrots.

A small portion of St. Nick's deer herd—mostly the younger set—had gone south and west last spring, rather than south and east to their normal habitat in Finland. It turned out that reindeer had a particularly low-brow sense of humor—even worse than most Delta operators. They liked spending their summers mingling with the Finnish herds and teasing them about not making the cut to become a Christmas reindeer. They also weren't above tripping them into mudholes and the like.

The breakaway herd had crossed down over the Canadian tundra, mingling with the caribou herds in some sort of convention. But they quickly grew bored as the Canadians had even less of a sense of humor than their Finnish counterparts.

That had led to any number of fights and endless head butting. The younger members of the herd whined about it no end.

"Teenagers," she scoffed to Horatio after he'd translated that for her. "Hard to deal with."

"Gift cards." Apparently that was his harshest epithet. "It is the only way St. Nick has found to deal with them at Christmas."

Betsy had been such a good girl as a teen, of course taking care of her ailing mother had made that an obvious choice. She'd even been well behaved as an Army grunt then a Delta operator. And now, just three days from freedom, she'd been injured and was drugged up in some Fort Bragg hospital. It didn't seem fair.

She tossed out some more carrots to get the rest of the story. Most had continued west to roam with the big herds in Alaska. But Jeremy had turned south once more, toward the heat and bright sun. He'd said he was headed to a place called Mont-a-land or something like. None of them had ever heard of it.

"Montana?"

Some of them thought that sounded right, but were more interested in carrots than answering questions. She took the bag with her when she left. When they protested, she simply made a show of resettling her rifle across her shoulders... which proved most effective. About time they did some growing up.

She and Horatio started in the Canadian Northwest Territories at a place with the unlikely name of Reindeer Station. Eight or nine houses located along the edge of the sprawling Mackenzie River delta less than fifty miles from the Arctic Ocean. It wasn't all that much warmer than the North Pole with just two days to Christmas. The river was iced over and was crisscrossed with snowmobile tracks. She'd borrowed a brilliant red parka with a white sheepskin lining to keep her warm.

It took most of the morning to track the region's sole remaining reindeer herder to his remote cabin. It was a gruesome affair. Not merely well away from even the hamlet of Reindeer Station, it was also the butchery for bulls thinned from the herd. Reindeer meat was stacked outside in the Arctic chill and quick-frozen beneath hides. Inside the hut, the tools of the trade dangled from hooks on the wall. Yet the herder also had a young reindeer on a leash as a pet.

Horatio was shivering even more than the temperature could account for.

Betsy held his hand tightly to calm him, which she didn't mind doing at all, while she was talking to the man. Even while shivering from disgust or distress, Horatio's hand was as warm as a handmade quilt. He appeared perfectly comfortable in his body-hugging leather despite the Arctic temperature.

The herder's English was limited and apparently Horatio was only fluent in English, French, and reindeer, so he was of no help. The herder, speaking mostly in some Inuit language, allowed as he might have seen a rather curious animal that had stood aloof from his herd of three thousand reindeer. A magnificent bull with more points than he could count. He waved south.

"Inuvik?" That was the next town, some twenty miles away.

He shook his head and waved again.

"Fort McPherson?" It was the only other town she knew in the Northwest Territories.

Again the wave south, "Mont-a-land."

CHAPTER 6

*B*ut going directly to Montana was too big a leap. It would take forever to pick up Jeremy's track again. So they worked south in stages following the rumors of an aloof, many-pointed bull reindeer.

"I thought Jeremy was supposed to be a cute little guy."

"Indeed he was, seventy-five years ago when Robert L. May wrote about him. He has matured somewhat over the years. He is still a sweetheart though as he never allowed the success to go to his head."

"How long do reindeer usually live? Maybe he died of old age."

"Fifteen to twenty years, typically, unless they are in the employ of St. Nicholas. Then their lives are rather extended."

Betsy eyed him carefully. There was an agelessness to Horatio's clear features. He would have been as classically handsome a thousand years ago as he was now. Perhaps there were some questions that it was better not to ask.

Besides, time was running too fast.

"Can't you slow it down?"

"Not even St. Nicholas can do that."

Thirty-six hours remaining.

Jeremy wanted her to eat something after they'd chased leads all the way down the frozen Mackenzie to the small town of Yellowknife on Great Slave Lake. From there, they'd run the ice road over to the hamlet of Detah and were now sitting in a small barn. The owner had told the story of the most "magnificent bull" he'd ever tracked while hunting. Best he'd ever seen, but apparently his shot had gone wild.

"Jeremy is very wily," Horatio's whisper had tickled her ear like a warm breeze.

She tried a carrot, but they'd frozen hard. "Give me an MRE and let's get going."

So, he gave her a pre-heated Meal-Ready-to-Eat. She didn't ask how. Next time she'd ask for a roast beef dinner with Yorkshire pudding and see if her friendly neighborhood hallucination could deliver.

"Maybe you should rest." The small barn had a hayloft, and the hunter had returned to his ice fishing on the frozen lake. It was tempting. So very, very tempting. She couldn't remember the last time she'd been this tired.

"When the mission is done." She chowed down on the Southwest Beef and Black Beans while Horatio massaged her shoulders. Now that was something she could become very used to—far better than the cold, lack of sleep, and the utterly ludicrous situation.

His fingers were strong enough to ease even her soldier-hard muscles until she felt ready to melt against him. She tossed aside the empty MRE package and decided that a little melting wasn't completely outside the mission profile.

She'd forgotten—mostly—about the kiss in the ancient French bistro. The memory did nothing to prepare her for what happened next. Horatio felt luscious as he pulled her tightly against him. In mid-clench, she tried to rub herself even more tightly against his incredible body.

Horatio grunted, and not in a good way.

"Your vest," he managed to gasp.

Betsy paused and looked down between them. She wore her Glock sidearm, as most Delta did, front and center for a fast draw. Above that, pockets of ammo and emergency supplies made hard edges that had left scrapes on his smooth leather.

"Sorry." Vest. Mission. Ludicrous scenario.

The only way out is through.

She sighed, sat up, and patted Horatio's cheek. He had the decency to look disappointed despite the gouges she'd been digging into his chest.

"Your colonel," Horatio nodded to the south, "said that you were the hardest-driving scout in his entire team."

"You spoke to Colonel Gibson about finding one of Santa's reindeer?" She tried to imagine how the stern colonel took it.

"Perhaps I may not have asked him quite directly, but he was very impressed with your skills."

That was news to her. She hadn't known that Delta Force's commander even knew who she was.

She sighed to herself that some overwound inner drive wouldn't even let her enjoy a hallucinatory snuggle.

They left the tiny Detah barn and they turned south across Alberta.

CHAPTER 7

They had pizza in Banff and she spent three delicious hours mostly passed out in the curve of Horatio's arms in a snowed-in hiking cabin high in Glacier Park. She didn't ask how Horatio moved them from place to place. It seemed that they flowed, glided, perhaps simply morphed from one destination to the next. It was a dream, so it was easy to not question the transitions.

But she would miss her time with Horatio. No, she'd miss Horatio himself. Even strung out on whatever narcotic was giving her this extended dream, she was becoming very attached to him.

Yes, he'd started out all strange and mysterious and mostly concerned about a missing reindeer. But he had shifted. More slowly than their jumping from one place to another, but just as steadily.

Still wrapped in her parka, she lay in his arms in the chill cabin and felt…right. As if it was where she was supposed to be. Perhaps "content" was a better word, though it was not one that had ever come up before in her life.

He hadn't asked about her past, which was just as well.

She didn't want to talk about it. But neither had he talked about his. Did elves have pasts? Did elves have regrets? She hoped not as she had enough for both of them.

"What is an elf's life like?" She could feel him shift as if he was looking down at the top of her head in some surprise.

"Normal enough. The reindeer usually do a good job of taking care of themselves, that's why I didn't think to worry. Generally I spend but one month a year tending them. It's a good life for them as well." And he began telling her about their grazing habits, and the practical jokes they liked to play.

One year they'd started at the South Pole rather than the North, forcing St. Nicholas to act like a Dumpster-diver as he dug out successive presents from the bottom of the sleigh's pile instead of working top-down. Or the year they'd switched all of the rabbits' stockings with all of the squirrels'—the rabbits had ended up have a grand game of ice hockey with the acorns and walnuts but the squirrels had never figured out what to do with the sudden bounty of cabbage.

It was only as they were trekking south into the Flathead Wilderness of Montana that she realized he'd told her nothing of himself. Perhaps it was fair, she'd said nothing of herself either, but it rankled. Of course, with his voice, she'd happily listen to him reading the naughty and nice name list —especially the naughty if he gave some of the details.

Dawn broke hard.

She couldn't think of how else to describe it. While traveling through Canada, they had been in and out of snowstorms beneath gray skies. This morning, they'd left the cabin in Glacier Park beneath the last stars of the night, almost as brightly perfect as those from Santa's reindeer stables. It had been a relief that the North Star had shifted well down the sky, so they were indeed well to the south.

But standing atop the Castle Reef ridgeline and looking

down at the Montana Front Range in one direction, and up into the heart of the snow-capped Rocky Mountains in the other, dawn began with a snap as sharp as the cold.

The sun lanced over the flat horizon from impossibly far away and the entire world was catapulted into a limitless blue bowl of sky.

"I take it this is why they call it Big Sky country," Horatio sounded breathless.

"I guess." Betsy also couldn't catch her breath. It might be the eight-thousand-foot elevation or the slicing cold of the morning wind driving ice crystals into her face like blowback from Barrett .50 cal sniper rifle.

It might be the view.

But it was more the realization that this was December 23rd. One way or another, their quest would be over today. As soon as sunset hit the International Date Line in roughly twelve hours, St. Nicholas would be flying off to do his job— with or without the errant Jeremy.

Yet she could feel that he was close. Some instinct, honed over the years by Delta training, told her their quarry was nearly in sight.

She flagged down a rancher passing by in his helicopter, who settled it neatly atop the peak. Clearly ex-military by how he flew, despite the fact that he now commanded a small Bell JetRanger with a herd of horses painted along the side.

"How can I help you, ma'am?" He drawled it out in a Texas accent so fake that it would get him lynched in certain states. "Need a lift off this here hilltop?"

"No, we're fine."

"We?" He tugged his mirrored sunglasses down enough to squint at her strangely.

She glanced aside at Horatio who just shook his head.

Fine. Whatever. So he was invisible or something. Had he shown up for anyone else, or had she just crossed Canada as a solo crazy lady talking to herself? She'd bet on the latter, but didn't have time to deal with it now.

"Have you seen a reindeer that—"

"Reindeer? We have moose and elk in these parts. Even a few caribou, but no reindeer."

"Reindeer and caribou are the same animal," Horatio prompted her.

When the pilot didn't respond, she repeated the information.

"Wa'll, ain't that a wonder."

"Have you seen a particularly impressive one lately?"

He rubbed his chin thoughtfully. He'd have been the handsomest man in any crowd that didn't include Horatio.

"Might have heard mention of one. Over to a hot spring up along the North Fork Deep Creek. My wife said she saw one when one of our guides and a guest shot—"

"Shot?" Betsy grabbed the pilot's arm in a panic.

"Shot two *young* bulls," the man looked down at his arm in some distress and tried to shake her off. At least the awful Texas accent was gone.

She shook him by his arm to keep him talking.

"She said it was the biggest old bull she'd ever seen. Had himself a couple of does and a fawn. Guess they didn't want to break up the family. Ease off, lady." He wiggled his arm a little and grimaced.

"Jeremy has a family?" Horatio's blue eyes were almost as wide as the Big Sky. Then he looked at her and his gaze shifted as if asking if she also had a family.

She had no one. No one on the outside, and in just another day, she'd be out of Delta and have no one on the inside either. This definitely was *not* the moment she wanted to be thinking about her future.

"Do you know where that hot spring is?"

Horatio nodded.

"Of course I do," the pilot looked at her strangely. "I'm the one who just told you about it. Are you okay all alone up here?"

"Not really." She let go of the pilot who began massaging the arm she'd had a hold of. She was hunting for one of Santa's reindeer and absolutely falling for a hallucination named Horatio, but she didn't want to talk about it with some rancher pilot. "But I can find it on my own."

"I can't just leave you here, lady." The pilot looked around. There was nothing to see from the summit of Castle Reef except snowy mountains, dusky plains, and the biggest blue sky ever.

"Fine, *I'll* leave *you*, then. Thanks for the help."

She walked past Horatio. For the first time, she could feel one of his spatial shifts slowly wrapping around her before it actually happened.

"What the hell?"

She liked that she left the pilot with his own hallucination to figure out. Misery loves company.

CHAPTER 8

The hot spring was unoccupied, but it didn't take her long to pick up the fresh tracks through the snow.

"By the tracks, it's a big bull, two does, and a half-grown fawn."

Horatio let her lead the way. It was a hard slog through the deep snow, even though the herd had broken the path.

At one point, an avalanche had erased their tracks. It took them several anxious hours to pick them up again on the far side of the damage path.

It was barely an hour to local sunset—and only four or five to Global Flying Time—when she found them. The small herd was grazing near a copse of Douglas fir that had blocked much of the snow. They were kicking aside the little snow that remained and eating the frozen grass.

"Jeremy!" Horatio's shout of joy shook loose an entire cascade of snow from one of the trees that she barely managed to dodge.

The two of them—elf and reindeer—ran to each other

and were soon chattering away in reindeer which sounded like grunts and squeaks to her untrained ear.

Betsy ducked under the low-hanging branches and found a small spot clear of snow where she could lean back against the trunk and wait.

Exhaustion rippled through her as it always did after a hard scouting job. But it wasn't just that. She was leaving Delta because she could feel that she was losing the edge and, with how far past it Delta normally operated, that was an unacceptable change. One far too prone to death. For the first time since she'd joined the Army, she didn't belong anywhere. Yet over the last three days…

Betsy watched Horatio as he was introduced to the rest of Jeremy's family.

For the last three days, Betsy had started to belong. Not merely due to her skills either. When she was with Horatio even something as crazy as searching for Santa's missing reindeer made sense. Anything…*everything* somehow made sense when she was with him. She hadn't truly belonged somewhere that she could ever recall, but she could see herself belonging with a fantasy named Horatio.

She must have dozed, though the sun had barely shifted when Horatio kissed her awake. That gained her undivided attention, but he was too excited for it to last more than a moment.

"He has a family. But he couldn't get them back to the stables on his own. He needed an elfin herder to transport them the first time. Jeremy is a good man—"

"Reindeer," she corrected him.

"Reindeer," Horatio readily agreed and kissed her on the nose. "He didn't want to abandon his family, but didn't know any of the locals who could send me a message. Apparently love at first sight happens for reindeer as well."

As well? Is that what had happened to her? It didn't seem

very likely, but neither did anything in the three days since she'd last stood on Range 37.

Now Horatio was looking at her very intently. "You're the most amazing human I've ever met, Betsy."

"Human?" But that said nothing of the amazing elf women he'd surely known. Why was she pining for a drug-dream fantasy?

"Woman. Of any breed or species. I've been watching you for days and can't believe your tenacity and skill. Or your beauty. Can all human women kiss the way you do?"

Betsy could feel herself becoming overwhelmed by his compliments. But nothing overwhelmed a Delta soldier. They were trained to keep their thoughts under control in any situation.

She slipped her fingers into his magnificent mane of hair and tugged it lightly to pull him closer.

"Perhaps I won't give you any excuse to find out."

"Mmm," he made a happy sound as he leaned into her kiss.

She could feel it supercharge her, ramp her up even the way a decisive victory couldn't achieve. There was a feeling of vitality, of joyous triumph at being alive at the end of a hard battle.

Horatio made her feel that ten times over. His kiss filled her thoughts until they overflowed and radiated back to him. She wanted him to take her right here, right now. Under the trees. In the snow. Even with the reindeer watching. She didn't care.

She opened her eyes to look up into his amazing eyes the color of the Montana Big Sky, just as a particularly large snowflake plastered itself across her shooting goggles she didn't recall putting back on.

It left a wet smear when she brushed it aside.

And once again she was in the heart of a mock Afghan village, dusted with North Carolina snow.

A mannequin bearing an RPG leaned out of a doorway.

Only habit had her shooting it twice in the face and once in the chest.

CHAPTER 9

*B*etsy finished the Range 37 course with the same high marks she always did, but felt none of the victory at the score—even though she'd managed to snatch-and-grab the bad guy on her own.

The next two days were a slow slog through the bureaucracy of leaving a service she'd given a decade to. Quartermaster this. Housing that. Personnel records the other thing.

She couldn't equate the Range 37 exercise and the two days of bureaucracy involved in leaving the service with the three days she'd spent with Horatio the Herder tracking a stray Christmas reindeer.

At each step she took through her Fort Bragg reality over the same three days, she could feel the other reality fading into memory. The three days with Horatio had passed so quickly and now time crawled.

December 21st: Quartermaster this. Horatio's strong hands resting on her shoulders a moment longer than needed as he helped her into a red-and-white parka while they stood in the most magnificent stables she'd ever seen.

December 22nd: Housing that. Holding each other close in a small hayloft in Detah on the frozen shores of the Great Slave Lake. A feeling of belonging she'd never known.

December 23rd: Personnel records the other thing. Waking in his arms in a Glacier Park cabin and knowing she had never been anywhere so safe or so…important before in her life.

December 24th: nothing but a blur. Horatio the elf would be with his reindeer, making sure they performed their annual flight, preparing the stable for their return. Bedding them down when they were done.

No one that she'd served with was currently rotated into Fort Bragg from abroad, so she passed her final days in the US military in silence. Alone.

The snow had melted and new teams were working their way through Range 37. No twelfth-century French village with bad wine and poisonous stew would be awaiting them any more than it was awaiting her. She'd go back if she could, just to see Horatio once more. Once she was out, maybe she'd take her motorcycle to Europe and go searching for a French pub with an Airborne shoulder patch carved into one table's surface.

But there wouldn't be. Hallucinations didn't work that way. It had taken a long and lonely Christmas eve to convince herself that was all it had been.

Early Christmas morning, she turned in her firearm, was issued her DD 214 Honorable Discharge form, and was issued a temporary visitor badge that would see her to the front gates. She bundled up against the chilly day, missing the warmth of the North Pole parka, though she didn't really feel the cold anymore. Climbing on her Yamaha YZF superbike, Betsy rolled out the Manchester Gate by Pope Airfield.

Maybe she'd swing south and see a bit of the country. She

had no real plans until summer. But then her course would be certain. This summer, she'd be chasing the melting snow north, starting with the Flathead Wilderness. Even if it hadn't been real, she'd retrace the path as far north as she possibly could, right up to Reindeer Station on the banks of the Mackenzie River.

Perhaps there would be a reindeer, a small fawn grown into the grand bull that would at least remind her of Jeremy and she could pretend that he would lead her north to a stable made of yew trees.

At the Fort Bragg gate, the corporal took her temporary pass, and saluted her smartly. She returned the gesture for the last time, then rolled out the gate. Out Manchester Road, she'd pick up North Bragg Boulevard and punch south.

For now.

Then she'd—

Betsy slammed on the brakes and tried to make sense of what she was seeing.

Just off base, along the wooded lane, stood Pyrates Sports Bar. It wasn't much of a place: pool, beer, and a decent burger.

And leaning against one of the big maples stood an impossibly thin man with black hair down to his waist and eyes the color of the Big Sky.

She couldn't release her death grip on the handlebars as Horatio strolled up to her and reached out to raise the visor on her helmet.

"Hi."

"Hi? *Hi!* That's what you have to say for yourself? I've spent three days convincing myself that you were just a hallucination. What are you doing to me? Is this some kind of weird drug experiment or—"

Horatio leaned in and kissed her.

She dropped the clutch. The Yamaha lurched then stalled,

and broke the kiss. She'd already forgotten his taste of cinnamon and the great outdoors. How had she possibly forgotten that?

"Does that feel like a hallucination in your consideration?"

Betsy could only shake her head.

"I know this is a little abrupt, but how would you like a job?"

"No way, Horatio. You evaporated at the end of the last one."

"I would not this time."

"And I'm supposed to trust an elf hallucination on that?"

"Absolutely," and Horatio's smile lit his eyes to a merry twinkle, just as they did every time.

"Why?"

"Because I could use the assistance of a skilled reindeer herder."

"You want me to live at the North Pole with you?"

"We would travel a lot. I only tend the reindeer around Christmas. An elf's main job during the year is rather global: spreading good cheer wherever he can."

"Can you promise me that you're not a hallucination? I really want you to not be a hallucination." Even if he was, Betsy had the feeling that she wasn't going to care.

"I've been wracking my brain to find an appropriate Christmas present for you. That wish will do nicely. I promise you that I am completely real."

She hadn't thought about a Christmas wish in a long time, but if there was ever one she wanted to come true…

Betsy kissed him lightly, then nodded toward the back of the bike.

"Climb aboard, Horatio. We've got some good cheer to spread."

CHAPTER 10

*B*etsy leaned against the yew tree that made one side of the stable's main door and pulled her red-and-white parka more tightly about her as she watched Horatio with the herd. It was Christmas Eve and once more the excitement practically shimmered through St. Nick's stables.

Harnesses with bright polished bells were laid upon well-curry-combed backs as the reindeer pranced with delight. A small elf choir stood up in the hayloft singing about Good King Wenceslas, Little Drummer Boys, and Friendly Beasts. She noted that Rudolph was nowhere in the repertoire— Jeremy was *not* a fan of Robert L. May. He'd grown to be a very dignified reindeer.

"Especially now that he has a family to look after," Horatio had whispered softly in her ear one night.

And his nose was definitely not red, his main point of contention.

Before Jeremy was harnessed into the lead position, he clopped over to her and faced her silently.

Betsy's grasp of reindeer language still sucked, though she was improving.

But he didn't say a word.

Instead, he tipped his head down, and shifted his face gently against her chest and simply rested it there. His great rack of antlers framed her protectively to either side.

She hugged him, wrapping her arms around his head.

"Merry Christmas to all," she whispered to him. "And have a good flight."

He snorted a soft laugh at her twisting of the last line of Rudolph's story before pulling away to stride over to his position to be harnessed in.

With a stamp and snort and a prance and a paw, the herd was soon aloft, towing St. Nick and his sleigh on their merry rounds.

The silence seemed to be a long time settling over the stables once they were gone. But in time, even the fireflies had settled and only the quiet stars of the Arctic night lit the stables.

Jeremy slipped close beside her and wrapped his arms about her. She rested back against him and marveled at how her life had changed. How she would never be alone again.

Last Christmas, Horatio had given her a gift beyond imagining, she was no longer alone in the world.

She rested her hand on her own belly.

Tomorrow, Christmas morning—after the reindeer had completed their flight, then gone to bed for the night—she would tell him the news.

Her gift to him would be—she tried not to think it in the same rhythm as the Rudolph poem, but being married to a Christmas elf was changing her in many wondrous ways— that quite soon they'd be three.

DANIEL'S CHRISTMAS
(EXCERPT)

IF YOU LIKED THIS, YOU'LL LOVE DANIEL
AND ALICE

*D*aniel Drake Darlington III pushed back further into the armchair and hung on for dear life. Without warning the seat did its best to eject him forcibly onto the floor. Only the heavy seatbelt, that was threatening to cut him in half he'd pulled it so tight, kept him in place.

"You never were the best flier."

Daniel glared at President Peter Matthews as Marine One jolted sharply left. They occupied the two facing armchairs in the narrow cargo bay of the VH-1N White Hawk helicopter. The small, three-person couch along the side was empty. The two Marine Corps crew chiefs and the two pilots sat in their seats at the front of the craft.

"I'm fine," Daniel managed through gritted teeth. "I just don't like helicopters."

President Peter Matthews sat back casually. Apparently all the turbulence that the early winter storm could hand out had not interfered with his boss' enjoyment of Daniel's discomfiture.

"And why would that be?"

The President knew damn well why his Chief of Staff

hated these god-forsaken machines. Even if Marine One was probably the single safest and best maintained helicopter on the planet, he hated it from the depths of his soul along with all of its brethren of the rotorcraft category.

"My very first flight. I suffered—" a jaw rattling shake, "a bad concussion. Then we crashed."

"Yes," the President stared contemplatively at the ceiling less than foot over their heads.

Daniel kept his head ducked down so that he didn't bang it there as they flew through the next pocket of winter turbulence.

"That was one of Emily's finer flights."

And it had been. If the helicopter had been flown by anyone of lesser skill than Major Emily Beale of the Special Operations Aviation Regiment, Daniel knew he'd have been dead rather than merely bruised and battered. Thankfully the Army trained the pilots of the 160th SOAR exceptionally well, even better than the four Marines flying the President's personal craft. And Major Beale was the best among them, except for perhaps her husband.

The tape of that flight and the much more fateful flight a bare two weeks later had become mandatory training in the Army's Special Operations Forces helicopter regiment. To this day he knew his life would have ended if he'd been aboard for that second fiery crash. The crash that had taken the First Lady's life a year ago.

But that didn't make him like this machine one whit better.

"There's home." President Matthews nodded out the window just like any tourist. Any tourist who was allowed to fly over the intensely restricted airspace surrounding the White House.

Daniel managed to look toward the window as the helicopter banked sharply to the left. Please, just let them land safely and get out of this storm. The White House did look terribly cheery. November 30th, she wasn't sporting her Christmas décor yet, but she was a majestic building, brilliantly lit, perched in the middle of the most heavily guarded park on the planet. Another jolt and he squeezed his eyes shut.

He did manage to force his eyes open as they settled flawlessly onto the lawn with barely the slightest rocking on the shock absorbers.

In moments the door slid open and a pair of Marines stood at sharp attention in their dress uniforms as if the last day of November were a sunny summer day, and not blowing freezing rain at eleven o'clock at night.

Daniel stumbled out and managed to resist the urge to kneel and kiss the ground. For one thing, it would stain the knees of his suit. For another, the President would laugh at him. Okay, he'd laugh even more than he already was.

Both feet on the ground, Daniel found himself. Managed to pull on his Chief-of-Staff cloak so to speak. He grabbed his briefcase and kept his place beside the President as they headed toward the South Entrance. They each carried umbrellas of only marginal usefulness that the Marines had thoughtfully provided. Now that they were on the ground, Daniel didn't mind the cold rain in his face. It meant he was alive.

"I'd suggest turning in right away, sir. We have an early start tomorrow."

The President clapped him on the shoulder, "Yes, Mom."

"Your mother is over in Georgetown."

"Well, I'm not going to call you 'dear' so don't get your hopes up there."

Daniel had come to really like the President. Even at the end of a brutally long day, including a flight to Kansas City, then Chicago, and back, he remained upbeat with that indefatigable energy of his. He was easy to like. There'd now be no oil workers' strike in Kansas City and his Chicago dinner speech had benefited the new governor immensely.

"You go to bed too, Daniel."

"Just going to drop off this paperwork," he held up his briefcase.

The President headed for the Grand Staircase and Daniel turned down the white marble hall and headed over to the West Wing.

Somewhere behind them in the dark, the helicopter roared back to life and lifted into the night.

Keep reading at fine retailers everywhere:
Daniel's Christmas

ABOUT THE AUTHOR

M.L. Buchman started the first of, what is now over 50 novels and as many short stories, while flying from South Korea to ride his bicycle across the Australian Outback. Part of a solo around the world trip that ultimately launched his writing career.

All three of his military romantic suspense series—The Night Stalkers, Firehawks, and Delta Force—have had a title named "Top 10 Romance of the Year" by the American Library Association's *Booklist*. NPR and Barnes & Noble have named other titles "Top 5 Romance of the Year." In 2016 he was a finalist for Romance Writers of America prestigious RITA award. He also writes: contemporary romance, thrillers, and fantasy.

Past lives include: years as a project manager, rebuilding and single-handing a fifty-foot sailboat, both flying and jumping out of airplanes, and he has designed and built two houses. He is now making his living as a full-time writer on the Oregon Coast with his beloved wife and is constantly amazed at what you can do with a degree in Geophysics. You may keep up with his writing and receive a free starter e-library by subscribing to his newsletter at: www.mlbuchman.com

Join the conversation:
www.mlbuchman.com

Other works by M. L. Buchman:

SIGN UP FOR M. L. BUCHMAN'S NEWSLETTER TODAY

and receive:
Release News
Free Short Stories
a Free Book

Do it today. Do it now.
www.mlbuchman.com/newsletter

Printed in Great Britain
by Amazon